HIGHLAND TERRACE ELEMENTARY SCHOOL
100 N. 160th
Seattle, Washington 98133

First published in the United States of
America in 2003 by
Walker Publishing Company, Inc.
First paperback edition published in 2006
Distributed to the trade by Holtzbrinck Publishers

For information about permission to reproduce selections from this book, write to
Permissions, Walker & Company,
104 Fifth Avenue, New York, New York 10011

The Library of Congress has cataloged the hardcover edition as follows:
O'Malley, Kevin.
Straight to the Pole / Kevin O'Malley.—[1st U.S. ed.]
p. cm.
Summary: A boy who is struggling through snow to get to school
is about to give up but then hears some good news from his friends.
ISBN-10: 0-8027-8866-1 • ISBN-13: 978-0-8027-8866-5 (hardcover)
ISBN-10: 0-8027-8868-8 • ISBN-13: 978-0-8027-8868-9 (reinforced)
[1. Snow—Fiction] I. Title.
PZ7.O526St 2003      [E]—dc21      2002192408

For EMILY

ISBN-10: 0-8027-9570-6 • ISBN-13: 978-0-8027-9570-0 (paperback)

The artist used watercolors on 240-pound watercolor paper to create the illustrations
for this book. Line work was created with a quill pen and blended Higgins inks.

Book design by Nicole Gastonguay

Visit Walker & Company's Web site at www.walkeryoungreaders.com

Printed in China

10 9 8 7 6 5 4 3 2 1

# Straight to the POLE

## Kevin O'Malley

**Walker & Company**

**New York**

Frozen and alone.

Pressing on
through the snow.

Pushing
through
the wind.

Over hills

and mountains.

SLIDING.

Bone-chilling wind
biting my cheeks.

must go on.

The ice and snow have
filled up my boots.

CAN'T . . . GO . . .

on.

Oh no . . .

A WOLF!

Lost and alone. . .

But wait,

in the distance,

# A RESCUE.

My friends

tell me that
school has been

closed for the day!

HOORAY!